J FICTION W (NEW) (P/T)

JAMES CHEATS!

BY **THALIA WIGGINS**
ILLUSTRATED BY **DON TATE**

magic
wagon

visit us at www.abdopublishing.com

Published by Magic Wagon, a division of the ABDO Group, PO Box 398166, Minneapolis, Minnesota 55439. Copyright © 2012 by Abdo Consulting Group, Inc. International copyrights reserved in all countries. All rights reserved. No part of this book may be reproduced in any form without written permission from the publisher.

Calico Chapter Books™ is a trademark and logo of Magic Wagon.

Printed in the United States of America, North Mankato, Minnesota.
102011
012012

 This book contains at least 10% recycled materials.

Text by Thalia Wiggins
Illustrations by Don Tate
Edited by Stephanie Hedlund and Rochelle Baltzer
Cover and interior design by Neil Klinepier

Library of Congress Cataloging-in-Publication Data

Wiggins, Thalia, 1983-
   James cheats! / by Thalia Wiggins ; illustrated by Don Tate.
      p. cm. -- (Making choices. The McNair cousins)
   Summary: James resents having to repeat the sixth grade in a class which includes his younger cousin Greg, so he turns to cheating to keep up with the work.
   ISBN 978-1-61641-633-1
   1. Cheating (Education)--Juvenile fiction. 2. Decision making in adolescence--Juvenile fiction. 3. Cousins--Juvenile fiction. 4. Schools--Juvenile fiction. 5. Resentment--Juvenile fiction. 6. Trinidad--Juvenile fiction. [1. Cheating--Fiction. 2. Decision making-Fiction. 3. Cousins--Fiction. 4. Schools--Fiction.] I. Tate, Don, ill. I Title.
   PZ7.W63856Jaj 2012
   813.6--dc23
                                        2011027714

C

Eeny, Meeny, Miny, Moe! 4

A Big, Fat F 13

A New Idea 19

A Decision 27

Birds of a Feather 32

Round Two...................... 37

A Little Help 43

Caught! 49

Hard Work 54

Making Choices: Greg the Good ... 62

Making Choices: James the Rock .. 63

About the Author................ 64

About the Illustrator 64

Eeny, Meeny, Miny, Moe!

"I wonder what's taking Greg so long," Grandpa said as he helped Charles to his feet. He grabbed Charles by the arm and allowed his grandson to lean on him.

"I don't know, but it should be him helping!" James sucked his teeth. He grabbed Charles's left arm. Both he and Grandpa helped Charles regain his balance and swing into the minivan.

"Man, you're getting heavy!" James complained.

"Believe me," Charles said as he eyed James from his seat, "I have it worse. I have to smell your stinky breath five days a week. Don't you believe in using toothpaste?"

April burst into laughter.

"That's enough," Grandpa warned. He turned and called up to the window of Greg's bedroom. "Hurry up, Greg!

We're going too be late." He and James carefully placed the wheelchair in the van.

"I don't care if we are late," James said. He hated that he was repeating the sixth grade because he got into serious trouble stealing last year. He knew plenty of boys who had repeated a grade or not even graduated high school, but he regretted that he was one of them.

Greg finally joined them in the van. "Grandpa," Greg began, "I thought about it and I don't want to skip to the sixth grade."

James was twelve and the thought of his younger cousin in the same grade as him gave him a stomachache. He felt that his friends were laughing behind his back.

"Nonsense," Grandpa said, smiling. "You're just nervous. You worked very hard last year and you were able to advance to the sixth grade. You don't think that's a good thing?"

"It is," Greg shrugged. "But I'm only eleven and the other kids will be bigger and the work will be harder."

"Don't be such a crybaby!" James told Greg. He placed his hands behind his head and leaned back on the headrest. "Besides, it's not so bad."

James couldn't understand why Greg wasn't happy.

"Yeah, because you're repeating the sixth grade!" April called from the passenger seat. "It will probably seem like a breeze." She started to laugh. "And Greg is in your grade. It must be embarrassing to repeat a grade but also to have your younger cousin skip *and* be in your classes! You must really be stupid!"

"Alright you two!" Grandpa warned.

As soon as Grandpa pulled up alongside the school, James hopped out without a word. James noticed that his friends weren't waiting for him by the front steps.

James brushed past Greg as they went inside. They passed the metal detectors and headed to their class.

James swaggered inside the classroom and noticed Moochie sitting in the corner. Moochie smiled and pointed to an empty seat right beside him. As James came nearer, he noticed that Moochie looked nervous.

"Man, I can't believe we have the same history teacher!" Moochie hissed in James's ear. "I heard Ms. Clemens is hard."

"Yeah," James nodded. "She's always trying to get us to study and learn. She says it's important and makes our lives enjoyable, blah, blah, blah! Don't worry." He patted Moochie on the back. Then he wondered what would happen if Moochie got better grades than he did.

"Okay, class." Ms. Clemens raised her hand to warn the students to quiet down. "As sixth graders, you will be graduating this year. In addition, you will be taking an important nationwide test." She paced back and forth between the desks.

"That does not include what we will be covering in my class. I believe that you all can do the work." When she eyed James she tried to smile. "I hope this means you too, James."

James shrugged and pretended to look interested.

"To see where everyone is in their learning, we will have a pop quiz." She walked back to her desk and picked up a small stack of papers.

"Right now?" Greg blurted. "On the first day of school!"

Several classmates murmured. Ms. Clemens continued to smile.

"Yes, Greg. Right now. In fact, we will have a series of quizzes throughout the school year."

Ms. Clemens handed several sheets of paper to each student in the front of

the rows. They passed them down to the students behind them.

James looked at his quiz paper. *What's the point?* he thought. *I'll never pass this quiz. I caused so much trouble last year.*

He looked around the room at his classmates. Moochie was trying to cheat off of someone's paper. Finally, James looked at Greg. *I bet he'll pass this. He's so smart! I bet he thinks he's better than me!*

James frowned at his paper. *I'll just guess. Eeny, meeny, miny, moe!* With that, he picked his answers.

A Big, Fat F

"Well, Rock, I failed!" Moochie laughed as the bell rang. The boys headed outside.

"I am so glad the first day is over!" James stretched his back. "I feel like shooting some hoops." He noticed Greg walking ahead with his head down.

James's friends had started calling him the Rock the summer before. When they all got in trouble together, they had bonded. Now the boys felt more like family to James than his own family did.

James signaled to his boys, and they signaled back. Silently, James and his friends crept behind Greg.

Without warning, James pushed Greg into Troy. They formed a circle around him.

"Man, I can't believe you skipped grades!" Moochie said as he pushed Greg into Troy.

"Yeah! You think you're so smart, huh?" Troy pushed Greg into James.

"Just don't think you're all that because you skipped. Don't even think about trying to help me with my homework!" James hissed in his face.

"Come to think of it, that may be a good idea," Troy chuckled. "If Greg is both the good and the smart cousin . . ."

"Then you're the bad and the dumb one!" Moochie added. "You might need Greg's help!"

His friends laughed. James noticed Greg trying not to smile. He felt the heat rise on his neck.

While James and the boys were stealing to earn money, Greg had been doing odd jobs around the Trinidad neighborhood of Washington DC. He had earned the community's respect and the nickname Greg the Good. Now, James was constantly being compared to his goody-two-shoes cousin. It made him very angry.

"Shut up!" James gave them all a look that made them quiet down. He pushed Greg to the ground. Before he turned to walk off, he gave Greg a look that meant trouble later at home.

The next day, Ms. Clemens handed back the graded papers. James pretended not to care when he got his.

I shouldn't be surprised to get an F, James reasoned. *I'm not smart anyway, so why try? I wonder what grade Goody-Goody Greg got.*

James waited for Greg to leave the classroom before he snatched Greg's quiz from his hands and pushed Greg against the wall. He could not believe that Greg had a D on his paper.

Yes! James thought. *Greg failed, too!*

James took in Greg's disappointed face. "Not so smart now, eh? Are you hoping that Grandpa will let you back in the fifth grade?" James smiled.

Greg tried to ignore him. As he walked away he shook his head and said, "I didn't know half of that stuff!"

James jogged up behind Greg and said, "You're actually getting worked up about a quiz? It's only the second day of school!"

Greg turned to him. "There is a lot of pressure on me to pass. Grandpa came up to my room last night and told me how proud he was to have one of his grandchildren skip a grade."

"Don't be such a crybaby!" James hissed.

As James walked away he couldn't help feeling both jealous of and confused by Greg.

Grandpa came to my room, too, James thought. *Only he told me how disappointed he was in me and how I could do better. Sometimes I wish he would get off my back!*

A New Idea

"Don't worry, Greg. I'm sure you will do much better on the next one." James overheard Ms. Clemens telling Greg. She handed back his second quiz paper. Greg groaned.

"Well, you did better than me, smarty-pants!" He displayed the fat F and *See Me* Ms. Clemens had written on his quiz. Greg did not look pleased.

That afternoon, James joined his friends at the recreation center's basketball court.

"Shouldn't we be studying?" Moochie asked as he started dribbling the ball.

"Man, you and Greg worry too much!" James stole the ball and headed down the court. He successfully did a layup.

"Maybe I can be a professional basketball player. It doesn't look like I'll do well in school," James said.

"Man, you're smart," Troy said as he guarded James. "You just need to focus."

"Focus on this!" James shot a three-pointer from where they were standing. Jeff, his partner, cheered.

"Nice!" Moochie congratulated him. "I guess you'll make a great ball player! In the meantime, I know of someone who might be able to help us."

"Who?" James stopped dribbling.

"The guy's name is Sonny. He sells cheat sheets. You know, the answers to quizzes and homework lessons that teachers reuse every year."

"Yeah, I've heard of him," Jeff added. "He's supposed to be good. He never gives out a wrong answer."

"Really?" James was too distracted to notice Troy heading down the court to score. James caught up to him in time to block the shot.

"How come I've never heard of him?" James frowned.

"Well, it's not like he wants everyone to know what he's doing," Moochie said. He tried a three-pointer and missed.

"Bend your knees more," James advised. "How do I find Sonny?" The ball rebounded off the hoop and he caught it.

"Put the word out," Moochie said. "He'll find you. When he does, have him meet us at my house." Moochie tried to get the ball from James. James blocked the attempt and shot another three-pointer.

James kept thinking about Sonny on his way home later that day. He felt bad about wanting to cheat, but he was tired of having Grandpa on his case demanding that he do better in school.

I don't know why he thinks I can be smart like Greg! What's the point? I'll never be as good as him, James thought.

James thought about Greg struggling to pass. *Maybe I should tell him about Sonny.* Then he thought of how everyone gave Greg special treatment because he skipped. *He should just suffer!*

James came into the kitchen and noticed Greg studying hard at the dinner table.

"I can't believe you!" James laughed. "All of this studying because you failed a couple of quizzes? You're such a nerd!" He yanked the book from Greg's hands.

"Hey!" Greg shouted.

James stood and held the book out of Greg's reach. "Ms. Clemens is so hard. You'll never get that perfect A. So why try?"

"Because," Greg got up and jumped for the book, "I like to know that I did my best. We have to pass both Ms. Clemens's class and that nationwide test! And I couldn't disappoint Grandpa!" He finally caught the book from James. James punched Greg in the shoulder before they both sat down.

James thought again about telling Greg about Sonny.

"Leave Greg alone and help me set the table," Charles said. He was having a hard time getting the pork chops out of the oven from his wheelchair.

James grabbed the pork chops and slammed them on the counter to cool. He told Greg, "I heard a boy named Sonny deals in cheat sheets."

"What?!" Greg and Charles exclaimed.

"Yeah. He's supposed to be good, too. Almost every time he gets the correct answers to teachers' quizzes and tests. Especially if the teachers recycle old lessons, like Ms. Clemens. Moochie told me about him. Strange I never met him before . . ."

Greg gathered his books and papers into a neat pile. He looked at James and said, "I'm not going to buy cheat sheets! I'm going to study hard and whatever grade I get will be the grade I earned!"

"Suit yourself, Greg the Goofy!" James shrugged. He stuck his foot out and tripped Greg as he walked by, nearly causing the books to drop. "But Sonny is hardly ever wrong. I'm gonna take a chance on him."

James grew angry with himself and Greg. *As usual, Greg makes the good decision and I end up having to make a bad one!* James thought as he ate his pork chops. *But what can I do? I have to pass!*

A Decision

James did not even look at his next quiz paper. He knew there would be another F and a note from Ms. Clemens about how he needed to talk to her.

I can't believe she told Grandpa about my grades and about some stupid study group. How would I look with a bunch of nerds?! James thought.

That afternoon he looked for Sonny. He went to the recreation center, the convenience store, and all of the apartment buildings where his friends lived or hung out. No Sonny.

"I'll put the word out that you're looking for him. Someone should know where he is," Moochie's older brother, Ken, told James.

"Thanks, man," James muttered. Then, he headed home. He was angry that he couldn't find Sonny.

I've got another test coming soon. James pounded his fist in his hand. *Where is this boy?*

James made his way into the kitchen. He pushed Greg out of the way and fell into a chair.

"Nice to see you, too," April said huffily. She didn't take her eyes off of peeling the potatoes.

"Whatever." James waved his hand impatiently. "I've been looking for Sonny."

April faced him. "Why would you want to meet with that rotten boy?" she asked. "Decided to go into another line of work and join him?"

James burst into laughter. "No. I actually want to buy a cheat sheet from him. Ms. Clemens called Grandpa and told him about my grades. Now I have to take some desperate measures."

Both April's and Charles's mouths fell open. James laughed again.

"You better not!" April shouted. "That boy is good for nothing. Besides, what if the sheet is wrong?"

"He's never wrong." James folded his arms.

"You buy a sheet from him and I *will* tell Grandpa!" April said.

James shrugged. "Well, I guess I can't buy one if I can't find him!"

"I mean it, James!" April turned back to mashing potatoes.

"I'll go with you," Greg whispered.

James could not believe what he heard. He turned to Greg and muttered, "Well, well! What a surprise, Greg the Goofy!"

"Whatever!" Greg hissed. "I just want to meet him and see what he is all about."

James smirked and helped Greg finish setting the table.

James still could not believe that Greg wanted to meet **Sonny**. *I guess I am a bad influence!* James smiled to himself. He felt better that even Greg wanted to cheat. He felt like Greg and he were equals now.

Birds of a Feather

Greg joined James at Moochie's door the following night. Moochie answered after the first knock.

"What's up, Rock?" Moochie and James bumped fists. Then he turned to glare at Greg.

"No trouble," James whispered in Moochie's ear. "He's here to meet Sonny."

"Oh." Moochie let them inside.

"You finally got in touch with Sonny, huh?" Moochie asked James as they sat down.

"Yeah. Turns out his brother hangs out with yours," James chuckled.

"Ahh . . . birds of a feather." Moochie joined in the laughter.

Suddenly, there was a knock at the door. The boys fell silent.

"Who is it?" Moochie demanded in a low voice.

"Yo, it's Sonny!" came a low bark.

Moochie silently opened the door. A boy taller than James slithered in. He looked over his shoulder as he came in, making sure no one outside noticed. He was dressed in all black. James took in Sonny's black trench coat and black hat.

Wow, James thought, *he must be a real hustler!*

"Y'all ready to do this?" Sonny quickly looked over the room and the boys.

"Yeah," James said. They all sat down on Moochie's couch. Sonny pulled out a file folder from under his coat. On

top was written *Ms. Clemens. Sixth Grade History*.

"You're sure that this is the next quiz?" James asked as he took the cheat sheet from Sonny.

"You want it or not?" Sonny demanded, snatching the sheet back.

"Chill." James smiled as he handed Sonny the money. "I heard you were good, but there's always the chance."

"Trust me." Sonny did not smile. He handed the paper back to James. He got up to leave and looked at Greg.

"What about you?"

James could tell Greg was tempted, but he didn't trust Sonny.

"No, I'm good. Thanks."

"Cool." Sonny shrugged. He handed James a piece of paper.

"This is my number. Make sure you call before nine or my grandmother gets upset." He bumped James's fist before he left.

"Man, that is one cool dude!" Moochie said, mesmerized.

"Yeah. He is so tough!" James agreed. He had a dreamy look in his eyes.

Round Two

"James, I'm surprised!" Ms. Clemens said as she handed James his recent quiz paper. "I knew you had it in you if you put in a little effort." She squeezed his shoulder encouragingly.

James ignored the pang of guilt in his stomach. He smiled triumphantly at the big A on the top of his sheet. He turned to grin at Moochie, sitting two desks over. Moochie grinned back, holding up his paper, which also displayed a huge A.

James caught Greg's eye and smiled gloatingly at him. James noticed that

Greg had another D on his paper. *Ha! Ha!* James thought. *All of that studying and for what? He still failed! I can't wait to tease him later!*

James caught Greg heading out the door and put him into a headlock. "What'd I tell you? Sonny pulled through! I'm going to get another cheat sheet from him tonight."

Moochie caught up to them. "Yeah, be at my house around eight."

Greg squirmed free from James's grasp. "I can't believe you two are doing this!" he hissed.

"We can!" James and Moochie said.

Later that night Greg followed James to Moochie's house. "So, are you going to get a sheet tonight or you just like following me around?" James demanded.

Greg didn't say anything. When Moochie opened the door, James pushed past him.

Sonny was on Moochie's couch playing a video game. Moochie went to join him.

"So you in, Greg?" Sonny asked without taking his eyes off of the screen.

"Um . . ." Greg mumbled. His throat felt dry. He looked at James, who nodded. "I guess so."

"Cool. It's ten dollars per sheet. Ms. Clemens's next quiz is a tough one, but I have all the right answers," Sonny said. "Now, where's your money?"

James and Greg hardly spoke on the way back to the house. James wondered if Greg would really read the cheat sheet he had just bought.

"I'm proud of you, Greg," James said as he put his arm around his cousin.

Greg shrugged his arm off. "Proud of me?! Whatever! I know cheating is wrong, but I want to do well."

"Well, you will. So, how does it feel to cross from good to bad?" James sniggered.

Greg did not answer.

Oh well, James told himself, *he'll be thanking me later when he starts passing!*

Later, James sat down to memorize his cheat sheet. He could not help the feeling that he was helping his cousin do a bad thing. And that *he* was doing a bad thing.

Why do I keep feeling miserable? James wondered. *I'm just helping myself along.*

Greg has decided to do the same. It's his fault he chose to cheat! He didn't have to buy the paper!

James kept feeling bad until he fell asleep.

A Little Help

"Great improvement, Greg!" said Ms. Clemens two days later. James watched as she hugged Greg. His jaw dropped at the big B on his paper.

James shouted, "Congrats, man! Nice to see you've improved!" He slapped Greg's back really hard. Several students laughed.

"James!" Ms. Clemens exclaimed. "Not so hard, please. I know you're as happy as I am that Greg is improving."

James tried not to laugh at Greg's face. Greg blushed red with anger. James knew Greg wanted to say something, but he didn't want Ms. Clemens to overhear.

Later that night, James sat at the dining room table, watching Greg memorize the cheat sheet they had just bought from Sonny. Greg finally grew angry and put the cheat sheet in his bag.

"This is the last one," Greg told James. James smiled knowingly at him. Greg ignored him and helped himself to the dinner cooling on the stove.

"You said that last time," James reminded Greg.

"Cheating is wrong!" Greg declared. He turned to James and continued, "Besides, we are just fooling ourselves. If we don't know this stuff, how will we pass the final exam?"

"Sonny will probably have the answers to that, too." James shrugged.

"What if Sonny gets caught?"

"You worry too much," James said, shoving collards into his mouth.

"Okay," Greg continued, "what about next year? The next teacher will assume that we know this stuff, so next year will be harder and we will have to cheat again and again!"

"Luckily, Sonny knows the teachers at the junior high school! He'll be rich before we graduate!" James joked.

"That's not funny." Greg shook his head. He slammed his plate on the table. Then he reached into his book bag and pulled out the cheat sheet. He ripped it into shreds.

"What are you doing?" James shouted in disbelief. He dropped his fork.

"I can't depend on Sonny for the rest of my life! I've got to depend on myself! If I cheat, I'm only cheating myself!" He turned to James.

"I am going to my room to study. You're welcome to join me. Tomorrow I am going back to the study group. I'm going to do my best and pass the sixth grade the right way!"

James rolled his eyes. "You're making a big mistake. You know Ms. Clemens is hard. It'll be a miracle if you pass!"

"If I don't then I will study harder next year!" Greg headed up the stairs.

"You're such a dummy! And I thought you were smart!" James yelled. "You'll regret this!" Greg did not say anything. James turned back to his food.

I can't believe it! Greg is going back to his old ways! James frowned. Then he wondered if Greg was doing the best thing.

Could I do it? James asked himself. *Could I spend the rest of my school days buying cheat sheets?* Then he thought about his grandpa and Ms. Clemens. *I'll never be that perfect student like old Goody-Goody Greg! This way, I will have a little help.*

Happy with his decision, he finished his plate.

Caught!

"I have some important news, class," Ms. Clemens announced. She stood in front of her class looking very serious. "I have received word that a young man named Sonny has been selling cheat sheets of my old lesson plans. So, I have decided to change my lessons around.

"Since I have no proof, I won't accuse anyone of buying the cheat sheets," she said.

James noticed she was trying her best not to look at both Moochie and him.

Ms. Clemens continued, "However, you can all be assured that cheating will not be tolerated at this school. Sonny is not only suspended but facing expulsion."

James gasped.

"I will be stepping up my lessons," Ms. Clemens said. "I hope many of you can keep up. We still have work to do. Don't forget that there is a study group that meets every other day in the library at lunchtime." With that, she began handing out new exam papers.

James looked over his paper and groaned.

When the bell rang, James headed into the hallway. Greg caught up to him on his way to the next class.

"You should come to the study group," Greg told James quietly. "You don't have to fail."

James wanted to hit him. "I am not going to study with a bunch of nerds! If I ever get my hands on that Sonny . . ."

"Suit yourself," Greg said, placing his exam paper in his folder. A red B sat at the top.

Grandpa came into James's room later that day.

"Ms. Clemens called me and said that you were doing so well and that all of the sudden you made a bad grade. Is there anything wrong?" Grandpa asked.

James remained silent as he folded his clothes.

"There's word that a boy named Sonny has been going around selling answers to the teachers' lessons. You wouldn't know anything about that would you, James?" Grandpa asked.

James's heart pounded. He knew if he told Grandpa the truth, he would be in trouble.

But Grandpa already knew the truth. He sighed as he sat down on James's bed.

"I know I have been encouraging Greg a lot lately. Maybe I've been putting you down a lot, too." He looked at his grandson.

That's for sure! James thought.

"That's because I know you can do it, James," Grandpa put his hand on James's shoulder. "Don't let your fears of the past keep you from moving on in your future!"

"I'll never be as good as Greg!" James shouted. He felt tears in his eyes. "So stop bugging me!"

Grandpa didn't take his eyes off of James. "Then be as good as you can, James!" Grandpa said. "I know you and Greg are different. I know you've had a hard life, but don't let that stop you from doing something good. And all that goodness starts with a good education."

James let the tears fall. They burned his cheeks. Grandpa got up and hugged him.

"I believe in you. But you have to believe in yourself," Grandpa said.

James sobbed into his grandfather's arms. He knew that Grandpa Joe loved him. James knew what he had to do.

Hard Work

"I'm very grateful that you were all here to help me," Greg told the study group. "With your help, I'm getting better grades and will be able to pass Ms. Clemens's class!"

"Me too," Alex said.

"Are we going to study or act like a bunch of girls?" James cut in, opening his book.

"Yeah!" Moochie joined in. He looked at his book as if he had never seen it before.

Greg smiled. He opened his book and glanced at his cousin.

"James, what's the answer to number seven?" Greg asked.

James looked hard at the study question then closed his eyes.

"Um . . . C," James said.

Everyone cheered.

"Whatever." James looked both angry and pleased with himself.

Just then, the end-of-lunch bell rang. Everyone gathered their belongings and headed for their next class.

In the hall, Troy and a small group of boys were looking for James and Moochie. Troy's eyes widened when he saw his friends leaving the library with Greg and the study group.

"So I guess Greg *is* giving y'all lessons!" Troy joked. He and the boys laughed.

James grabbed him by the collar. Everyone stopped laughing. Troy looked scared.

"No more jokes!" James said calmly, "Maybe Greg could help you with your spelling! Even I know you don't spell *pitiful* with two p's!"

Everyone laughed except Greg and Alex. James looked at Greg and winked, then let Troy go. James put his arm around his cousin and together they made their way to their next lesson.

At the end of the quarter, everyone was looking forward to a break. The McNair family was having a cookout to celebrate everyone's report cards.

"So, Greg, is your school year all that bad?" Grandma Rose asked. She handed April a plate of ribs to pass down to James.

"It is challenging," Greg admitted. "But I learned that hard work will pay off in the end."

James rolled his eyes. Grandpa noticed.

"You weren't so stuck up when you saw that C on your report card, James," Grandpa said. "I've never seen such a big smile on your face! And I hope you continue that extra effort."

James rolled his eyes and shrugged. He caught Greg smiling at him. He smiled back and kicked him under the table.

James was proud of his hard work. He knew he would never cheat again. His grades weren't as good as Greg's, but he was on his way!

The End

Making Choices
Greg the Good

Every decision a person makes has a consequence. Greg the Good made some good and some bad decisions. Let's take a look:

Decision: Greg chose to stop cheating and study hard.

Consequence: Greg earned his grades and learned the material.

Decision: Greg chose to help his cousin study.

Consequence: Greg passed sixth grade with James and felt good about helping.

Making Choices
James the Rock

Every decision has a consequence. James the Rock made some good and bad decisions. Let's take a look:

Decision: James chose to cheat.

Consequence: James disappointed his grandfather and was further behind in his lessons.

Decision: James and Moochie decided to join Greg's study group.

Consequence: James earned a passing grade and got to move on to seventh grade!

About the Author

Thalia Wiggins is a first-time author of children's books. She lives in Washington DC and enjoys imagining all of the choices Greg and James can make.

About the Illustrator

Don Tate is an award-winning illustrator and author of more than 40 books for children, including *Black All Around!*; *She Loved Baseball: The Effa Manley Story*; *It Jes' Happened: When Bill Traylor Started to Draw*; and *Duke Ellington's Nutcracker Suite*. Don lives in the Live Music Capitol of the World, Austin, Texas, with his wife and son.